FA

D0656793

First published in 2008
by Franklin Watts

Text © Martin Glynn and Deborah Smith 2008
Illustrations © Oliver Harud 2008
Cover design by Peter Scoulding

Franklin Watts
338 Euston Road
London NW1 3BH

Franklin Watts Australia
Level 17/207 Kent Street
Sydney, NSW 2000

A CIP catalogue record for this book
is available from the British Library.

ISBN: 978 0 7496 7713 8

Printed in Great Britain

Fran

Bad Brother

Spike T. Adams

Illustrated by Oliver Harud

W

FRANKLIN WATTS

LONDON•SYDNEY

Chapter 1

So there I was. In my bedroom.

The bedroom I now had to share with him.

My heart was beating fast. I was breathing hard through my nose. Couldn't believe it!

My new trainers...

My latest grime-mix CD...

On Alex's bed.

Alex, my so-called step-brother, was using my things!

I was well vexed.

I had warned him the day he moved in:

"Stay away from me. And stay away from my things!"

He just wasn't hearing.

Alex walked in.

I felt my insides burning.

I wanted to put him in his place.

"What ya doing with my things?"

At first, he just looked at me.

Then he said, "I was tidying up the floor. I was gonna put your stuff back when I was done."

He thought he was smart. Trying it on.

But I ain't stupid.

I grabbed Alex up against the wall.

I could see he was scared.

"Touch my things again and I'm gonna bust ya ass," I hissed.

I wanted him to open his mouth so I could fill it with my fist.

But he didn't. He just kept looking at me.

Lucky for him I heard the front door open.

I pushed his face away. Didn't wanna risk getting cussed.

"Ya got away with it this time," I said.

I kissed my teeth and walked out.

It felt good.

Chapter 2

I made my way to the skatepark.

Wednesday is always packed there.

Rival crews meet to skate off.

Sometimes things kick off. But mostly, we get on.

Me and my crew, we were tight. A bit like
50 Cent's 'G' Unit.

We weren't gangstas. But sometimes we acted
like we were.

We were the 'T' Crew.

Coz everyone's name started with a T:

Me, Tyler — and then Tony, Tyrone, Tariq...

Tenisha, Tracy... And Talia.

I liked Talia.

Really liked her.

Talia was down with everything the 'T' Crew did.

And trust me, she looked good.

I knew that if we hooked up, we'd be so tight.

She smiled up at me.

I could smell her perfume.

It made my heart race.

The time felt right.

I was going to ask her...

Then she dropped it.

"Where's Alex?" she asked.

I was gutted.

It was me she should be checking.

I kissed my teeth.

"Why ya asking me? I ain't his keeper!"

Everyone turned around and looked at me.

I stared hard at every last one of them.

One by one they went quiet.

"Are we skating or what?" I snapped.

The crew stopped off at the chicken shop.

Zee was in there.

He's older, runs with a different crew, but we're cool.

I stayed back, chilling with Zee.

I figured if I stayed out long enough, Alex would be in bed when I got back.

Me and Zee talked on a level for ages.

A police car slid past.

We touched fists and went our separate ways.

"What time do you call this?" Mum snapped.

"I just forgot the time," I lied.

"No you did not!" Mum yelled. "This is about Alex. Why can't you be nice? It's hard for him - living somewhere new."

Nice!

I had to give him half my space!

That is more than nice.

I hate it when she cusses me out.

She went on and on and on.

Her man just sat there, saying nothing.

But his eyes were on me.

I wanted to cuss him — ask what he was looking at.

I turned and walked up the stairs.

Chapter 3

Next day at school it was hot. Things got better.

Trust me. Talia looked sweet.

She just kept smiling at me.

Not at Alex.

At me.

She threw a ball of paper. Teasing me.

"So you wanna mess?" I said, smiling back.

I threw the paper ball back at her.

I knew I was gonna get in trouble.

But it would be worth it.

"So we're linking at The Dome tonight, yeah?"
I asked the crew.

Talia nodded. "Gotta do my stupid French
homework first."

She rolled her eyes. "Gonna take me ages."

"I can help you lunchtime, if you want. I'm OK at French."

It was Alex.

Trying to sneak in and cosy up with Talia.

Just cos his mum's from Dominica, he thinks he can speak French.

"Thanks, Alex!" Talia beamed at the creep.

"You'll come to The Dome tonight, yeah?"

Smiling up at him.

Big brown eyes shining.

I couldn't believe it.

She was asking him out.

To come and meet with my crew.

And I had to stand there and watch it.

It made me sick.

Alex had a big, stupid grin on his face.

"Sure. Thanks," he said.

I wanted to hurt him so badly.

Chapter 4

No way was I walking to The Dome with Alex.

I left the house on my own.

I was angry.

Why did Talia ask him to come?

The Dome is the 'T' Crew's special place.

And Alex ain't in the 'T' Crew.

Never will be!

Tonight I was gonna make it plain.

People are either down with me — or him.

I pulled the boards back over the secret entrance.

Wasn't gonna help him find his way in.

Let him figure it out, if he's so clever.

Maybe he'd cut his hands on the nails.

Or maybe fall through the rotten stairs.

He won't know the safe bits to tread on.

Serve him right.

"Yo!" I called out

Everyone came over to touch fists.

Bwoy! Talia looked fitter than ever.

She sure had made an effort.

She drives me crazy.

Tariq put a can in my hand.

"Borrowed from your old man?" I asked him.

Tariq grinned.

His old man sells booze in his shop.

He moans that "a lotta teefin's goin' on".

My phone rang.

I looked at the screen.

It showed Alex's name and number.

I kissed my teeth.

The phone kept on ringing.

"Tyler, aren't you gonna answer that?" Talia asked.

"It might be Alex trying to get in."

"It ain't," I told her.

I switched the phone off.

Chapter 5

He turned up anyway.

Looking all mashed.

Talia went over to him.

"What happened to you?" she asked, all concerned.

She began brushing the dust off his jacket.

Now she felt sorry for him. That was all I needed.

I downed the rest of my can.

"You want a drink?" Talia asked him. "You look like you need one."

I watched as she gave him a can.

She even opened it for him.

I was vexed!

I went over and grabbed the can out of his hand.

Started drinking it.

"What ya gonna do now?" I said to him. "Talk to me in French?"

Some of the others laughed.

Talia rolled her eyes.

I was waiting for some response.

Nothing! He said nothing.

Just stood there looking like a wimp.

I wanted to mash him up there and then.

He didn't even have the bottle to stand up to me.

I hated him even more.

He's weak, man.

Good job he ain't my real brother.

Chapter 6

A couple of the crew began throwing some moves.

They called us over.

One thing I know is I can dance.

And then I remembered.

At that family party last month?

Alex just stood there, watching.

I bust two moves and kicked it.

"So Alex, you gonna join in?" I asked.

I could see he didn't like it.

"I don't dance," he mumbled.

"Come on Alex, just move ya body!" Talia said.

The whole crew was dancing now.

But not Alex.

I knew I'd got him this time.

I went over.

"See Alex, it's like this," I said.

"Being smart is one thing. Being cool is another. And right now, you ain't cool."

"Why do you keep shaming me up?" he asked. Quiet, so only I would hear.

I just kissed my teeth and carried on moving.

Alex began to walk away.

The rest of the crew was too busy showing moves to notice.

"Run off, then!" I called.

"You don't belong with this crew.

Your name don't fit — and your face don't either!"

He didn't look back, just kept on walking.

Good! Now he knew his place.

I ran things here. Not him.

The partying went on.

"Alex left then?" Talia asked, dancing up close.

I shrugged.

"You blazing him all the time," she chided.

I pulled her to me.

She seemed to like it.

Her perfume was making me dizzy.

"Can you hear that?" Tracy called.

"That's a police siren," Tenisha said.

Talia pulled away. "What? Coming for us?" she said, alarmed.

I pulled her back. "It's going somewhere else," I told her.

"No, Tyler, it's getting closer," said Tony. "It's coming here!"

He was right.

The siren scream was getting louder by the second.

"Yo! Time to run!" I called.

We just picked up our things and exited the building.

Chapter 7

Outside, we huddled in the shadows, hiding.

"Looks like something serious," Tracy said in a shaky voice.

"Look! Someone's up there," Tariq pointed out.

We all looked.

"Oh, my God — it's Alex!" Talia said.

My insides felt heavy, like stone.

It was Alex, up there.

"What's your name son?" a policeman called up.

Alex said nothing.

The policeman went again.

"Come on, son. There's people out there worried about you."

Alex shook his head.

"And there's people who will be glad if I ain't around no more. So don't play me like that!" he shouted.

I could feel Talia was eyeballing me.

I couldn't look back at her.

"Listen young man, just stay calm," the policeman called.

"I don't want to stay calm any more!" Alex yelled.

He leaned forward as if he was gonna do it.

Everyone gasped.

"No!" I shouted.

I ran up to the policeman.

"His name is Alex. Let me talk to him," I said.

"And who are you to him?" the policeman asked.

I paused, big time.

And then I said it.

"I'm his brother."

Chapter 8

The policeman took me to the roof.

Alex looked really scared.

My own heart was beating fit to bust.

"We won't come any closer, Alex. Just relax," the policeman said.

"Do you want a drink or anything?"

Alex shook his head. "What's he doing here?" he asked, looking at me.

"He wants to talk to you," the policeman told him.

Like I couldn't speak for myself.

Alex looked away.

My mouth felt dry.

"Don't do this, Alex," I said.

He kept looking away. "Why do you care?"

His voice was flat. Like he had given up.

But Alex went on talking.

"I didn't ask my father to marry your mother.

I didn't ask to share a room with you.

Joke is, I always wanted a brother.

But look what happened when I got one."

He rubbed his eyes.

I saw one of his fingers was cut.

He must have done it getting into The Dome.

Cos I ignored his call.

I had to find the courage.

To say what needed to be said.

"Alex. I'm sorry."

Alex just stood there.

Then he looked around. His eyes were wet.

It was my turn to look away.

"You coming home then?" I asked.

"I'm freezing my arse off on this roof."

Alex made a noise. I wasn't sure if it was a laugh or a sob.

Didn't want to know.

All that mattered was that...

...slowly.

Really slowly.

Alex stepped back from the edge.

Jay has always wanted to roll with a cool crew.

To drive fast cars and have a hot girlfriend.

Then his dream comes true.

But will his dream burn up in smoke...

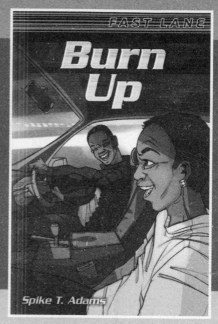

978 0 7496 7714 5

More titles by Spike T. Adams:

978 0 7496 7715 2

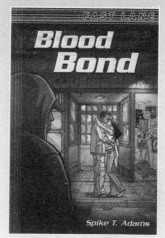

978 0 7496 7712 1